I PROMISE

written by LeBron James
illustrated by Nina Mata

HARPER
An Imprint of HarperCollinsPublishers

ISBN 978-0-06-297106-7

The artist used Adobe Photoshop to create the digital illustrations for this book.

Typography by Rick Farley

20 21 22 23 24 ROT 10 9 8 7 6 5 4 3 2 1

❖

First Edition

To the kids that started it all, my I PROMISE families in Akron.
These promises are for you, and I hope they may be helpful to every student,
classroom, and family across the country. You all inspire me each and every day!

—LeBron

To Aria and the kids who dare to dream bigger.
It all starts with the promises you make to yourself.

—Nina

I promise to work hard and do what's right,
to be a leader in this game of life.

I promise to go to school
and read as much as I can,

to follow the rules
and respect the game plan.

I promise to run full court
and show up each time,

to get right back up

and let my magic shine.

I promise to be open and try new things

and enjoy the happy that change can bring.

I promise to wear a big smile
and use kindness when I speak.

To remain strong yet humble
with every win and defeat.

I promise to ask for help
whenever I need it.

To reach for my star, even when I can't see it.

I promise to
ask questions

and find answers,

to believe in next time
and second chances.

I promise to use my voice and stand up for what's right.
And when things get tough, to keep up the fight.

I promise to stand tall, rise up,
and give all that I've got.

To throw the alley-oop
and uplift others on the spot.

I promise to respect my elders and peers the same.
To leave new places better than I came.

I promise to stay true, keep my head up, and never give up . . . no matter what.

I promise to dream big
and love bigger.
To be a team player
and a winner.

I promise to cross bridges,
and break down walls,

to rise with the sun
and learn from the falls.

I promise to be courageous,
to be free,
to strive for greatness . . .

to be me.

THE LEBRON JAMES FAMILY FOUNDATION

Your Promise

The I PROMISE School was inspired by the big dreams of kids in my hometown and around the world. It is a place committed to helping them and their families reach their full potential. At the start of every school year, and repeated each morning, all students make a set of promises to themselves just like those in this book. Setting goals, working hard, and holding yourself accountable are the first steps to success. We're excited to have you join in this journey to achieve your goals. Here is our daily promise to get you started!

Remember:
Nothing is given.
Everything is earned.

LeBron James

I PROMISE . . .

- TO GO TO SCHOOL.

- TO DO ALL OF MY HOMEWORK.

- TO LISTEN TO MY TEACHERS BECAUSE THEY WILL HELP ME LEARN.

- TO ASK QUESTIONS AND FIND ANSWERS.

- TO NEVER GIVE UP, NO MATTER WHAT.

- TO ALWAYS TRY MY BEST.

- TO BE HELPFUL AND RESPECTFUL TO OTHERS.

- TO LIVE A HEALTHY LIFE BY EATING RIGHT AND BEING ACTIVE.

- TO MAKE GOOD CHOICES FOR MYSELF.

- TO HAVE FUN.

- AND ABOVE ALL ELSE, TO FINISH SCHOOL!

#StriveForGreatness